The TOMTES
of Hilltop Farm

BRENDA TYLER

Hilltop Farm was a fine old farm with many buildings
and lots of animals, but it wasn't making enough money.
Farmer Robinson was so worried he put the farm up for sale.

Jamie and Emily, who lived nearby in Hilltop Cottage, often went to the farm to help their friend Dan, Farmer Robinson's son.

It was Dan's job to feed the animals. The goats were very naughty, so were the hens, and Bella the cow was ill.

"Will you help me stack the straw bales in the barn?" Dan asked his friends.

Then two smart men from the city appeared to look around the barn. The children hid and listened.

"When we buy the farm, we can knock this down and build a huge shed, where we can keep hundreds of animals in cages," one of the men said.

"Poor animals, locked up indoors!" cried Dan. "We can't let these men buy the farm. But what can we do?"

"We can go and ask our friends the Tomtes who live in the wood," suggested Emily.

Do you know about Tomtes? They are very rarely seen – never by grown-ups. They are happy to help around a farm, so long as they and the animals are treated with respect.

"Here I am," whispered Lichen, one of the Tomtes. "Can I help?"

"Oh, Lichen, Hilltop Farm is going to be sold to some men who won't look after the animals properly."

"Alack and welaway! I will ask my friends to come and help. You can help too. If you put on these Tomte caps you will become small like us, so no one will notice you."

That evening, the Tomtes came down to Hilltop Farm.
They told Dan and Jamie how to look after Bella.

The next day, Lichen and Emily
started to mend the fences and gates.

Lichen also explained matters to the hens.
"You must lay your eggs in the proper
place, not all over the farmyard."

The Tomtes and the children stopped the goats from eating leeks in the vegetable patch.

The next day was warm with spring.

Everyone sowed and planted all
sorts of vegetables: potatoes, beans,
lettuces, courgettes and tomatoes.

Next, they milked the goats,
and made goat's cheese.

"We will need baskets to carry everything down to sell in the town," said Lichen. So they all sat in the wood and made baskets of different shapes and sizes.

Soon it was time to pick berries. The Tomtes
gathered wild blackberries and blueberries
in the wood to surprise their friends. They
planned to take to them to the market to sell
alongside the farm goods.

Farmer Robinson noticed how well behaved the animals had become, and how many new crops were growing in the fields.

When he looked in the pantry, he was amazed to see fresh cheese, eggs and vegetables.

He was so grateful, he didn't ask where it had all come from.
"We have enough now to take to the market!" he said.

That evening, the Tomtes lit
their lanterns, ready to troop
down the hill to the town with
their baskets of berries. The
squirrels helped.

There were many customers at the market.
   "Such fresh vegetables," they said, "and delicious cheese."
   The wild blackberries and blueberries were very popular, and soon everything was sold.

"Hilltop Farm seems to be prospering again," said Farmer Robinson to his family. "I think we should give it another chance." He took down the FOR SALE sign.

"Thank you for helping us save the farm," said the children, as they handed back their Tomte caps.

"We will stay on watch and make sure all is well," said Lichen.

"And we will go on being good workers," said the children.

Lichen moved into the top of the barn with the old barn owl, to keep an eye on things.

From then on, Hilltop Farm flourished, though Farmer Robinson didn't know why. Dan and Jamie and Emily kept the secret of the Tomtes.

For Archie and Woody

First published in 2012 by Floris Books
© 2012 Brenda Tyler

British Library CIP data available
ISBN 978-086315-906-0
Printed in Malaysia